www.mascotbooks.com

Melvin the Sad...(ish) Robot v1.5

For more information, please contact:
Mascot Books
620 Herndon Parkway #320
Herndon, VA 20170
info@mascotbooks.com

Library of Congress Control Number: 2016912913

CPSIA Code: PRT0418B
ISBN-13: 978-1-63177-936-7

Printed in the United States

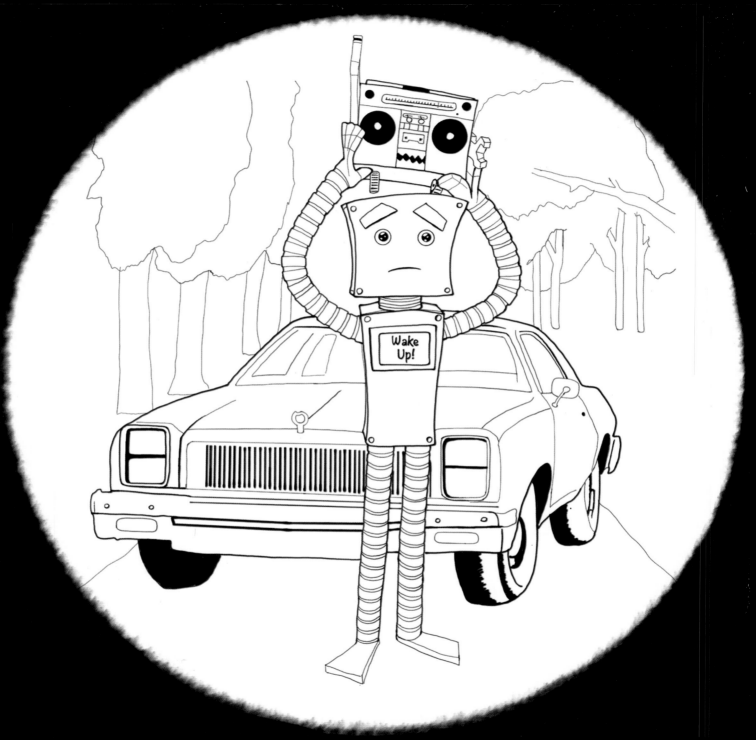

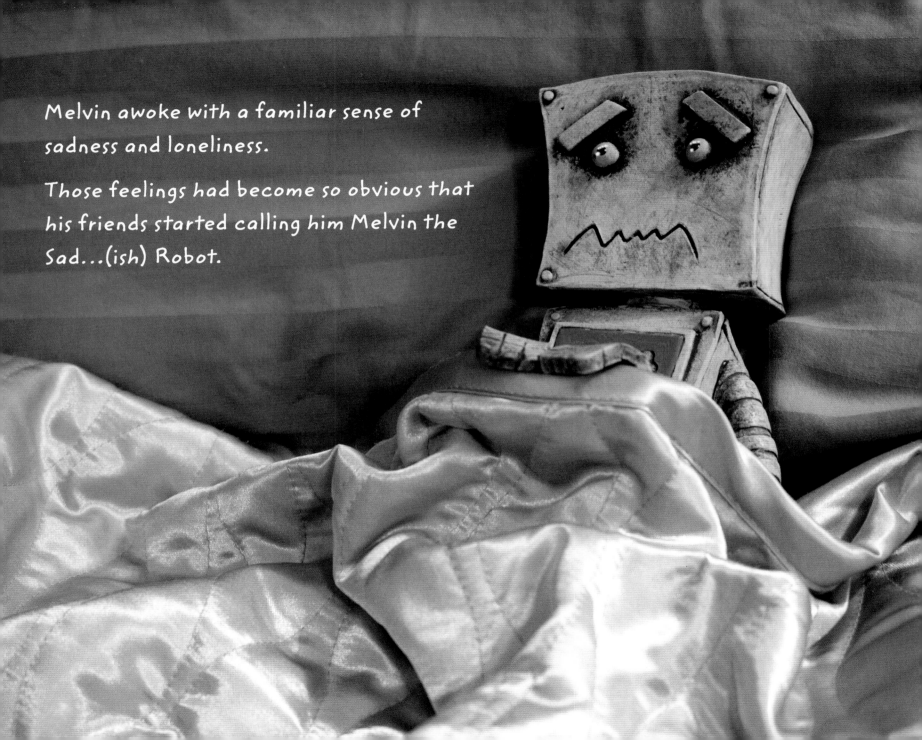

Melvin awoke with a familiar sense of sadness and loneliness.

Those feelings had become so obvious that his friends started calling him Melvin the Sad...(ish) Robot.

Each morning, he peeled himself out of bed and got ready for his day.

At school he was studying to be a "Fixer Bot," a robot who repairs other robots.

One day, on the way to school, Melvin ran into his friend Larry.

"Hey Melvin! Do you think you can help put my arms back on? They fell off...again."

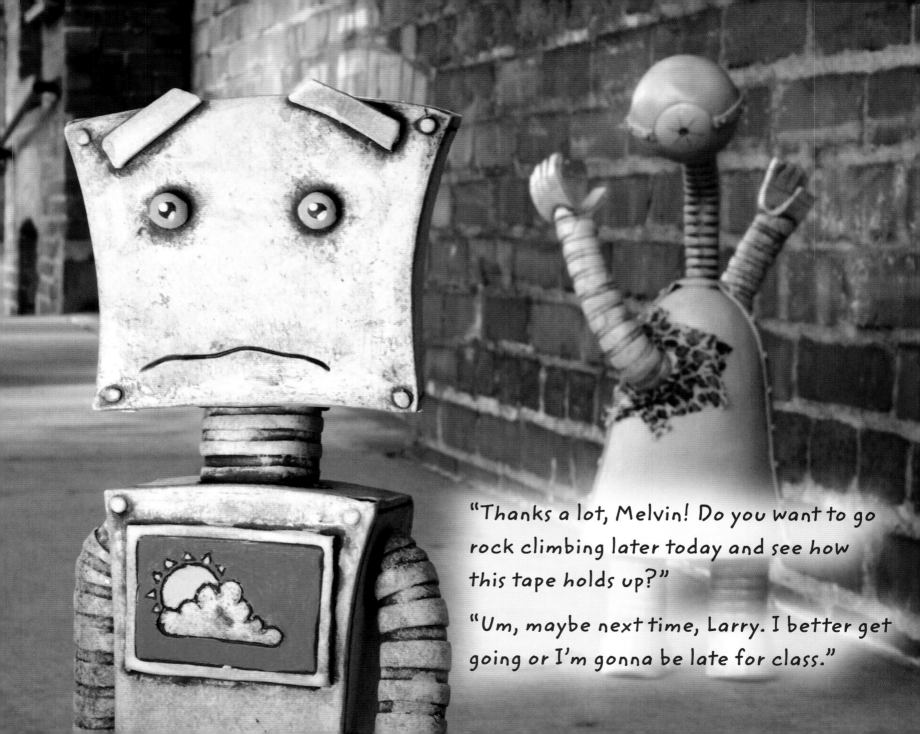

"Thanks a lot, Melvin! Do you want to go rock climbing later today and see how this tape holds up?"

"Um, maybe next time, Larry. I better get going or I'm gonna be late for class."

"Wait a minute! Is that a..."

"...Ladybug bot!?"

Did Melvin dare speak to her? Fearing rejection, Melvin began to run in the opposite direction.

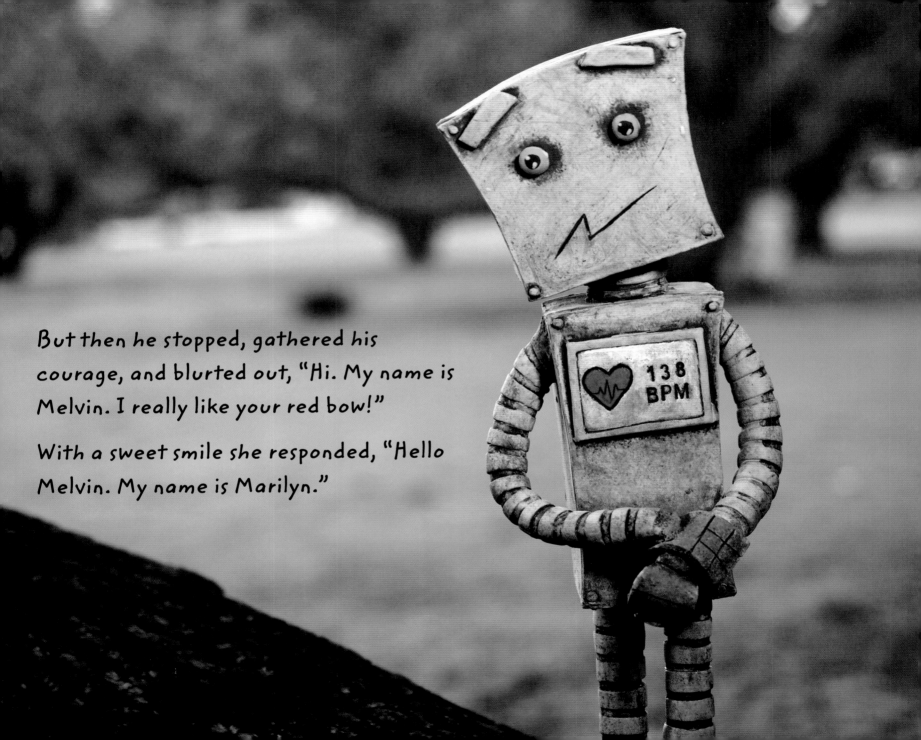

But then he stopped, gathered his courage, and blurted out, "Hi. My name is Melvin. I really like your red bow!"

With a sweet smile she responded, "Hello Melvin. My name is Marilyn."

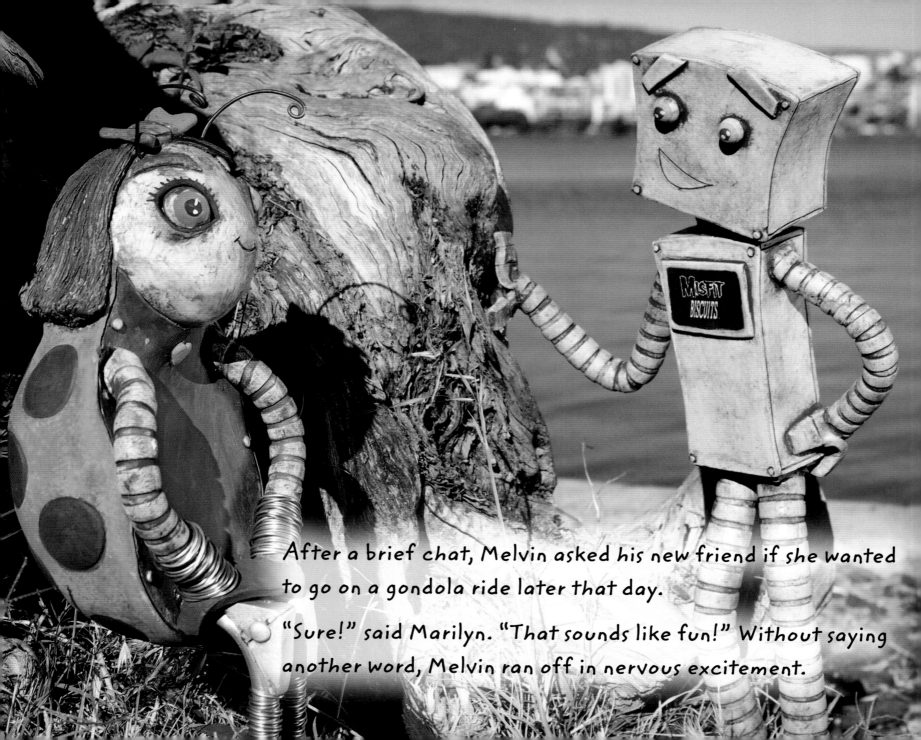

After a brief chat, Melvin asked his new friend if she wanted to go on a gondola ride later that day.

"Sure!" said Marilyn. "That sounds like fun!" Without saying another word, Melvin ran off in nervous excitement.

Melvin was noticeably distracted when he arrived at school, rambling to his lab partner Albert, "...and she has the coolest antennas."

"Um, isn't today's lesson supposed to be about fixing me?"

At home, Melvin computed the finishing touches to his outfit.

He arrived early and waited what seemed like a lifetime for Marilyn to show up. As a robot who lives forever, this was a really long time.

Discouraged, Melvin thought,
I guess she's not coming.

Why can't anything ever go right for me?

As he sulked back to his empty apartment, Melvin cried out, "I give up!" to no one in particular.

Suddenly, Melvin was knocked to the ground by a pack of wild creatures.

"Hey Melvin! Thanks for stopping these guys for me. I need to get them back to their foster homes soon."

"Have you ever thought about adopting a pet?" Larry asked. "I think you would love having a new friend in your life. They keep you super busy!"

Since adopting B.T.,
Melvin awoke to lots of
snuggles and burnt toast
each morning.

He still had his moments of sadness,
but he rarely felt lonely anymore.

And new friends were waiting around every corner...

"Melvin! You ran off so fast last time! I had no idea where we were supposed to meet. Aaand, you never told me you had a toaster dog!"

"Her name's B.T.," said Melvin. "Would you like to pet her?"

With B.T. at his heels, Melvin no longer feared trying new things. He was excited to take on each new adventure and live life to the fullest.

Melvin now had the opportunity to love and be loved, to experience new dreams and challenges, and most importantly, to be happy...(ish).

The End

This book is dedicated to the loner, the misfit, and the one who sees the world through different eyes. I am you, and you are me. We are together in this and the world will eventually start to make sense. Hang in there.

I would like to thank the following people for their help in bringing this book to life. Michele Karplak, for putting up with everything from a nugget of an idea to helping with photos and editing. My parents Martha and Jay Margolis, for encouraging and supporting me through everything. Han, Xine, and Al Lee Green, for help with photographs and dog wrangling. Hunter Rose, I know you can't read this, but this story is for you. The dog crew, Larry, Steph, Ji, Nacho, Stacy, Naomi. David, Robin, Natalie, and Ben Edwards, for being my first family of fans. To all my dedicated students for listening to me constantly talk about and bounce ideas off of you, and supporting me with your enthusiasm. A huge shout out to Reggie Chew and Stan Walker, as well as all my other amazing KICKSTARTER backers. To all the others who I have met along the way, who have given me encouragement, enthusiasm, and inspiration. Thank you.

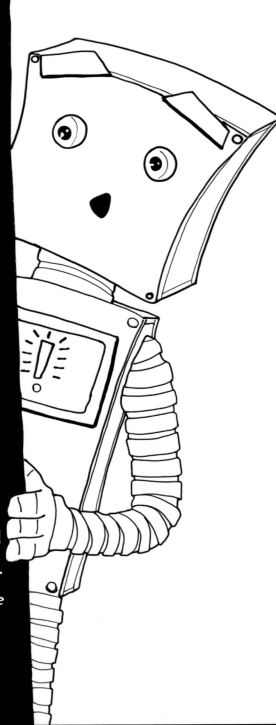

Joshua Margolis is an artist and educator living in the San Francisco bay area. By day, he spends his time teaching ceramics to the children and adults of San Francisco, and by night, he works on creating monsters and robots out of clay. His work has been shown in many galleries throughout the country, and can be seen each First Friday at his studio FM in Oakland, California.

Lake Merritt
Oakland, Ca.

Contact Joshua Margolis:

melvinthesadrobot@gmail.com

For coloring books, stickers, pins, and other extra goodies visit my web page at:

www.joshuamargolis.net

Instagram @clayandwine

Coming in 2019

Melvin
the Lost Robot